7/10

First published in the United States, Great Britain, Canada, Australia, and
New Zealand in 2010 by North-South Books Inc., an imprint of NordSüd Verlag AG,
CH-8005 Zürich, Switzerland.
Distributed in the United States by North-South Books Inc., New York 10001.

Library of Congress Cataloging-in-Publication Data is available.
ISBN: 978-0-7358-2296-2 (trade edition)
Printed in Belgium by Proost N.V., B 2300 Turnhout, November 2009.
1 3 5 7 9 • 10 8 6 4 2

www.northsouth.com

FSC
Mixed Sources
Product group from well-managed
forests and other controlled sources

Cert no. BV-COC-070303
www.fsc.org
© 1996 Forest Stewardship Council

THE Giant Wheel

By Andre Usatschow

Illustrated by Alexandra Junge

NorthSouth
New York / London

One evening, after the zoo had closed for the day, the animals decided to visit the Giant Wheel that had just been built next door. Everyone was excited.

"Is it true that from the top you can see the whole world?" asked Victor the crocodile.

"Oh, that would be wonderful!" said Samuel the tiger. "I haven't seen my home for years."

"All clear!" announced Peter the hedgehog, who had been sent to scout the way.

TIGER

One by one, the animals crawled through a hole in the fence and scrambled to the Giant Wheel. Peter, who was mechanically minded, climbed into the control booth. He pressed the green button and jumped into the nearest gondola. The gondola lurched back and forth, then slowly started to climb higher and higher.

HOT FRIES

NO ENTRANCE

TICKETS

"Wow!" shouted Peter. "I can see half—no, wait—I can see the *whole* city from here." There was the river that ran through the forest. There was the village where his grandfather lived. And there was his grandfather!

Peter was so excited, he couldn't sit still. He waved his scarf in the air and began to dance, hardly noticing that the gondola was already on its way back down again.

In the next gondola was Eska the polar bear.
He had been brought to the zoo when he was only a
cub, so he hardly remembered the North Pole, where
he had been born.

There was the cold blue sea and the glistening ice.
From here it looked as if the world was covered in
sugar. There were the northern lights glowing in the
sky and two walruses swimming in the icy water
without even a cap to keep their heads warm.

"Brrrr." Eska felt the cold north wind blow through
his fur.

When Victor got to the top of the wheel, he saw
Africa in the distance. A caravan of camels was
crossing the hot yellow sands of the desert. And there
was Uncle Neil in the river where Victor had been
born. Uncle Neil worked as a ferryboat, carrying
people back and forth across the river.

"Hallooooo!" Victor shouted at the top of his lungs,
waving his hat in the air. But his uncle didn't hear him.

Samuel was nearsighted. He was afraid he wouldn't recognize his own jungle, but it was easy to spot. There were thick vines and leaves and bamboo everywhere. Apes were swinging from tree to tree, screaming and throwing banana peels at one another.

"Their manners are just as bad as ever," Samuel muttered, but secretly he was pleased that nothing had changed.

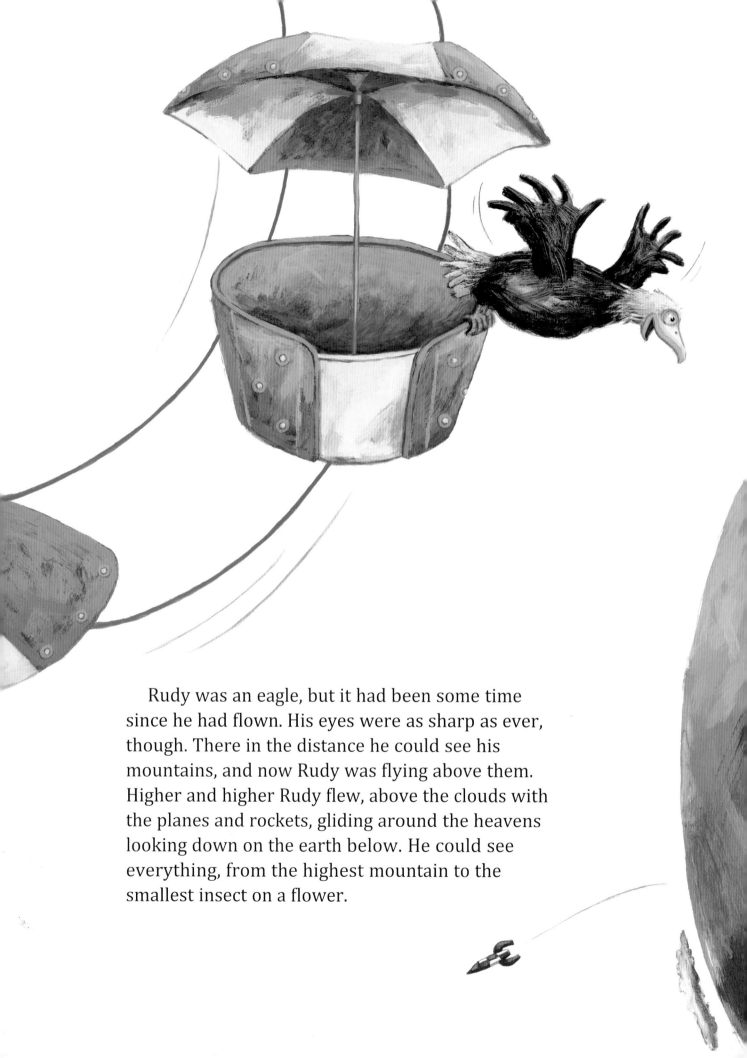

Rudy was an eagle, but it had been some time since he had flown. His eyes were as sharp as ever, though. There in the distance he could see his mountains, and now Rudy was flying above them. Higher and higher Rudy flew, above the clouds with the planes and rockets, gliding around the heavens looking down on the earth below. He could see everything, from the highest mountain to the smallest insect on a flower.

"Oooooh!" they sighed.
"Look at that!"
"Did you see what I saw?"

Just then, Leopold the zookeeper came out of his office and discovered that his zoo was empty! Where were all his animals? He ran to find Philomena the giraffe, who occasionally worked as his lookout. But Philomena was nowhere to be found.

Leopold grabbed his binoculars. All he could see was the Giant Wheel.

"I could get a good look around from the top of that wheel," he thought, and he hopped into the next gondola.

"Where are all the animals?" Leopold muttered, almost in tears as he looked up and down the streets. The higher he went, the more he saw. Soon he could see the whole country, and then not just the country but all of the countries in the whole world. Leopold was overwhelmed.

And then he looked down and saw the
animals jumping one by one out of the
gondolas and disappearing one after another
into the bushes. Leopold was so happy to see
them, he forgot to be angry.

"Maybe I'll just go around one more time,"
he thought. "Who knows when I'll have the
chance again!"

HOT FRIES

PLEASE DON'T
FEED THE ANIMALS

Happy knowing that all his animals were safely
back in the zoo, Leopold went round on the wheel
once more while the animals drifted off to sleep,
dreaming of their adventures on the Giant Wheel.

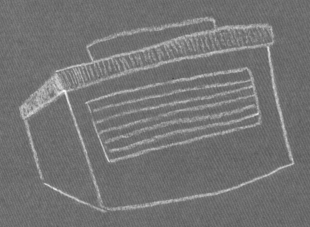